BIG RoSIE

Glenview, Illinois • Boston, Massachusetts • Chandler, Arizona Shoreview, Minnesota • Upper Saddle River, New Jersey

Big Rosie sat on a hill.

Rosie can spot a lot.

She can spot Jack and Dan.

Rosie can spot Rita.

She can spot Pat and Lucy.

Rosie can spot Melvin.

Gabriella is with him.

They zip past Kat and Pete.

Is it Ted and Izzy?

Look at Max jump.

Will Big Rig get him?

Rosie can spot a lot.

But can Dan and Jack?

Can Pat, Ted, and Max?

Will Big Rig hit Melvin?

Will the trucks bam, bam, bam?

Rosie can not look!

The trucks did not hit!

They did not bam!

But it was fun!

8